The illustration on the cover is from a painting by Paul Couchman.

Paul told us: "I have been painting and drawing since I was a child, and it has always been there from school, then through the difficult times in my life, such as being a full time carer for my parents until they died. Now working in London in the civil service in changed circumstances, I still paint. It helps me get through and will remain with me always."

To contact Paul about his work e-mail: plcouchman@yahoo.co.uk

Tales from the Buzzard

In 2009, Leighton Buzzard Writers were given a
grant to produce an anthology of local writing
about the local community, landscape and heritage.
A year on we are proud to unveil this collection of
prose and poetry; read on to see the results...

Leighton Buzzard Writers

Tales from the Buzzard; A Leighton Buzzard Anthology

A collection or prose and prose by Leighton Buzzard Writers

First published 2010

Copywright Leighton Buzzard Writers

ISBN 978-1-4461-2335-5

www.lbwriters.org

Tales from the Buzzard

A Leighton Buzzard Anthology

A collection of prose and prose by

Leighton Buzzard Writers

Foreword

Walking the dog across the Ouzel water meadows, an evening chill in the air, I considered how fortunate residents of Leighton Buzzard are that these water meadows survive and perhaps will survive into the future as their very purpose as nature's flood plains prevent urban development. Fortunate not just for dog walking convenience, but as a imprint of nature's landscape on the doorstep, a place it makes no sense to 'win' against nature's intention. Or does it? The canal, a feat of 19th century engineering, ploughs its course through the fields, and next to it, its cousin the railway.

Every story has at least two sides. A viewpoint is just a viewpoint. Fifty years from now, I'm confident that Leighton Buzzard will still be here and also the Ouzel meadows. But will people in Leighton Buzzard still write? I hope so, whatever the mechanism that transforms their thoughts into words. Writing is about sharing what it is to be us, to be people in our world, whether our words are about the past, the present or some imagined place or future.

What matters now is that enough people in this place, at this time, had enough they wanted to say that made this book come together: a celebration of this town, whether or not the pieces of work are positive. Writers may wear rose tinted glasses or they may not, but they all see their world through the lens of their own experiences. Given this fact, we can look upon this book as a kalediscope, looking at Leighton Buzzard from the top of All Saint's spire to the depths of the soul; a magical fairground organ that lets us see, hear and taste the flavour of where we live now.

If we enjoy the words in this book, or take something from them, then our thanks, first and foremost must go to the writers. Without them this would be a book of blank pages. But secondly we must thank the engineers: Leighton Buzzard Writers, a thriving writers' circle, for having the vision and the will and the time, and Leighton Linslade Town Council, for providing a grant allowing the project to get off the ground. In particular, thanks must go to Hannah Simpkins, Kevin Barnham, Rebecca Ridgway, Vanessa Byham, Mike Moran and Mark Norwood, the members of Leighton Buzzard Writers who gave up their free time to do the practical stuff that made this book happen.

Kate Allan
Leighton Buzzard
10th October 2010

Contents

The Book

By Derek Hardman

Take care, before creaking open.

For, once released, the printed words leap to the eye,

Escaping the confines of the pages,

Revealing the magic world

Trapped within the covers.

It sighs, softly, when closed,

Remembering escaped images.

Confession

By Derek Hardman

He knew he wasn't drunk as he stumbled out of the ASK restaurant, but was aware that he'd had his fair share of wine with the meal. It was 10pm, Christmas Eve, and the parties were just starting up in the pubs, but they were not for him. The sound of carol singing from the High Street reminded him of times past, before it all went wrong, and he stood silently, leaning against the restaurant wall, the better to hear. Tears welled in his eyes, as the wine took effect. The carols played with his imagination, and the thoughts of what might have been haunted him.

"Twenty-odd years" he thought, "Twenty-odd years. I was such a fool then, such a silly, young, fool; I should never have done it."

He slid slowly down the wall on to his haunches, and put his head into his hands. He thought back to the night when his life had changed. He'd been here in the town centre with his mates, and he'd had a few too many. He couldn't remember how the row had started, but he certainly knew how it ended. Both the town centre church and his life had been nearly razed to the ground, and ever since he had not been able to rebuild the latter. For the past twenty years or so, he had refused to admit his guilt, fought to be normal, and failed miserably, his soul burned beyond repair.

"I should have confessed all those years ago" he thought, "but everything's changed since then, apart from the guilt I've carried around. Why, even this restaurant wasn't here then, it was the old Fire Station."

The guilt had made him old before his time, and he knew that, because of it, his life had been cursed. As he squatted next to the restaurant wall, head fuzzy, hands and face now really cold, he was aware of someone standing in front of him. He knew it was a woman, for he could see that her skirt reached down to her ankles, and her shoes were quaintly buttoned up the sides. He looked up to see her dressed in what could only be described as old-fashioned clothes. A shawl was around her shoulders, and on her head a lace-trimmed bonnet was tied under the chin with ribbon.

"I must have drunk too much wine," he thought, "I can't quite make out her face." She spoke to him, her voice soft and gentle.

"It's time to face your demons, sir, and give up your secret; you cannot go on as you are. Do what your conscience tells you, and all will be well."

"But who are you, and what..." He broke off as the woman before him slowly started to fade away, and was gone in a few seconds. "Although I've had too much wine," he mumbled, "It's a sign. I must sort my life out, once and for all."

He got to his feet and lurched into the High Street, past the Market Cross, and stopped under the arcade in front of Boots chemist. All around him were families in festive mood, nodding and smiling at strangers. Children clattered excitedly about at the fringes of the carol singers, the Salvation Army Band huffed and puffed, and Rotarians in fluorescent yellow tabards shook buckets and handed out warm mince pies. He felt, as always, on the outside.

He stumbled along, determined on his destination, but deciding that he would progress in stages, the first of which would be Woolworths. He shook his head to clear out the fog, remembering that Woolworths was no more, another indication that time had moved relentlessly on without him. He moved slowly down the High Street towards Church Square, his mind now a kaleidoscope of images. Red felt Santa hats with white fluffy bobbles, brightly coloured glittering tinsel, rosy red cheeks, Fair Isle knitted gloves, wellington boots; all combining with people to create this special night of the year.

He reached the end of the High Street and paused as he entered Church Square, then looked up. Highlighted by spotlights, and towering magnificently over the town was the spire of All Saints Church. His jumbled mind cleared for a moment, as he realised that his sad life was as nothing compared to this church, here for nearly nine hundred years. His tears flowed, his heartbeat quickened, and he realised that this was his goal.

He had returned.

He made his way across the square and walked slowly up the church path, until he was inside the church porch. He had been here only once before. He knelt down, feeling the coldness of the frost which now covered the stone floor. For the first time in his life he clasped his hands in front of him, and, with a muted background of carols, prayed.

"Lord, forgive me. I was young, brash, and drunk, and agreed to show my companions what I thought of churches. I was wrong, and have suffered for it. Please, please, forgive me for starting the fire."

He was found in the same position, frozen to death, by the vicar who came to prepare for midnight mass.

"I can't say I know this man," said the vicar, "But I must say I have never before seen a face of such complete peace."

Through a Child's Eyes

By Shar Roselman

I live in a town with a funny name,
Mummy says it's called Laid on Buzzard.
If a buzzard is a kind of ignormous bird,
was it squashed when a giant laid on it?

I live in a town with a very tall spire,
But I'm glad our church is in Linslade
'cause Daddy says All Saints needs lots of rest or rayshone,
and I think that means the roof is falling down.

I live in a town with a map like a spider.
My teacher says seven streets run from the centre:
Stoke, Heath and Plantation, I can't remember the rest
but I know there are lots more roads than that!

I live in a town that holds fairs and celebrations.
I like spinning in teacups and the coconut shy
and watching the floats as they go by,
but I want to wear hats in Easter Bonnet competitions.

In my town there's a canal and the Little Ooze River.

Mummy takes me and my brother to feed the ducks

but sometimes Eddie cries when the geese hiss and cluck.

Then we race away laughing, and I always win.

I live in a town with its very own theatre.

I've seen Snow White and Buttons, and Tinkerbell's light,

but I sit near the back when Captain Hook has his fight

'cause his water pistol is the worst wetting of all.

I love living in a town called Laid on Buzzard.

Oops. Daddy's just told me, I've got it wrong,

Lay ton Buzzard is where I belong.

Is the buzzard so big it weighs a whole ton?

Decoding the Leighton-Linslade Parish Coat of Arms

By Damien Plummer

Entering and exiting Leighton Buzzard near St Christopher's garage, you, like me, probably pass the Leighton-Linslade heraldic Coat of Arms without noticing it, not realising its rich and interesting history. I'll explain it as I go.

Heraldry stems from the 12th Century when knights and nobility needed to be identified in tournaments and battle; it filtered down from landowning magnates (barons and nobles) to 'gentlemen' by the 15th Century.

First, the Shield: the Shield is a Metal then a Colour (this echoes its original practical construction). It is quartered Gold (Or) and Red (Gules) (both of these bracketed words are old French) meaning its bearer was a man of rank and also a magnanimous warrior.

Adopted by the 2nd Baron of Bedford, Payne de Beauchamp, on his marriage to Rohese de Vere, widow of Geoffrey de Mandeville, Earl of Essex, he took Geoffrey's Arms and adapted them: as Geoffrey on marrying Rohese had taken and adapted the de Vere's!

His father, Hugh, the 1st Baron, was a Norman adventurer (his surname 'Beauchamp' means 'Fair Field' – a common place name in Normandy and Picardy) who 'won big' after the Battle of Hastings in 1066.

Owning 43 Manors in Bedfordshire, he held three estates in Buckinghamshire (the Linslade being the largest in Buckinghamshire: a substantial estate of 15 'hides' where a 'hide' was a 120 acre mix of arable, meadow, pasture and woodland from 1068) and lands in Hertfordshire, taxed in the 1086 Domesday Book. By 1086 he was Sheriff of Bedfordshire, custodian of Bedford Castle and in 1086 was made Baron of Bedford by William I.

Notable De Beauchamps included: son Simon, benefactor of St Albans Abbey and witness to King Stephen's Charter of Liberties to Oxford; grandson Miles, who held Bedford castle against King Stephen 1137-8; but most famously, great-grandson William.

The 3rd Baron, he helped force King John to sign the Magna Carta in 1215 and for this was excommunicated. Restored to royal favour, he was the hereditary almoner at Henry III's coronation. Rebelling again against his King, however, he joined Simon de Montfort on 4th August 1245.

Everything surrounding the shield is called 'the achievement of arms'.

The helmet reflects the person granted the Coat of Arms. Thus for the De Beauchamps as Knights and Barons, it would be open and facing. This is exchanged for a 'tilting helmet' for Leighton-Linslade Council Officials who as private citizens, are gentlemen/gentlewomen ('esquires').

Around the helmet is the 'mantling' representing the cape or cloak the knight wore to protect his armour. Alternate red and gold, it counterpoints the Beauchamp shield.

Above the helmet is the twisted wreath reflecting the shield (gold and red) on which sat the Crest (traditionally the Animal, Bird or Monster identifier for the knight in tournament or battle).

Due to Leighton-Linslade being a Civic body, the Crest is complex. Above the wreath are two walled crowns representing land held on behalf of the king: Leighton Buzzard was held for Henry II by the Abbess of Fountevrault of Anjou in 1164. The De Beauchamps pledged Knight's Fee (personal military service to the King – e.g. William de Beauchamp in Wales in 1210 and Gascony in 1245 - and provided men for the Army at cost for 40 days) for all lands (and thus manors) held.

Golden cogs issuing from the crowns represent the modern industry present when the Coat of Arms was awarded: these included Sand (Garsides), Motoring (Camden Motors), Side Loaders and Lift Trucks (Lancer Boss) and Tiles (Marley Tiles).

Above is the Crest: a bird, not the Water Ouzel but the Mistle Thrush. Its medieval name was 'Ouzel' punning the river running between Leighton Buzzard and Linslade. Named for its love of mistletoe berries, it is said to be courageous enough to sing into the teeth of a gale: its other name 'Storm Cock' is apt.

The emblems on the shield are called 'charges' and divide it 'top', 'middle' and 'bottom' . The 'top' and 'bottom' charges represent our two most historic churches: All Saints Church in Leighton Buzzard and St Mary's Church in Old Linslade ('Old' separates the manor from the 'new' residential estates).

At the top, for All Saints, is one red and one gold celestial crown, representing heavenly reward. Built in 1288, it houses the famous 15th Century 'Simnel' carving. Its West Door's ironwork is by Thomas de Leighton who made the surrounding grille for Queen Eleanor's (Edward I's consort) tomb in Westminster Abbey at the cost of £13.

At the bottom, are alternate gold and red lilies: the lily is the Madonna's flower so is apt for St Mary the Virgin Church, parish church for Linslade built by Simon de Beauchamp, son of Hugh, in 1166. Largely rebuilt in the 14th Century, the 1913 Royal Commission states the Chancel Arch, North and South Nave and West Tower were 14th Century and the Church condition was 'good much restored'.

A bridge in the middle of the shield 'links' the towns and shows the powers of a Magistrate: Leighton has its own Magistrates Court. The wheat ear on the capstone, the fertility of Leighton-Linslade: Leighton's market stems from the

11th Century, with Henry III awarding a Charter to William de Beauchamp for a Linslade market in 1251.

Interestingly, the Coat of Arms for the local RAF Unit, RAF Stanbridge, features the Leighton-Linslade bridge. Stanbridge manor was granted to Hugh de Beauchamp in 1100 – 1118 by Queen Matilda, wife of Henry I.

So why did Leighton Buzzard and Linslade join? Initial 1961 boundary changes approved by the local Government Commission led to a Ministry of Housing and Local Government Official Inquiry with joining by Parliamentary Order on 1st April 1965.

In January 1966 the Leighton-Linslade Urban District was granted the Coat of Arms I've just described by the Duke of Norfolk, the hereditary Earl Marshal (who issues Letters Patent for all Coats Of Arms) on behalf of the sovereign.

The Summer of '63

By Keith Rawlings

I sat in the hotel bar, waiting for her. I hadn't seen her for a while, but she was a creature of habit and her weekday habit was 6.30pm in the seedy bar of the Railway Hotel; a cheap meal and too much booze until she was thrown out. She breezed into the bar with the confident air of someone who knows precisely where they are going. She scooped a menu off a table on the way to a barstool and put the menu flat on the bar as she sat down and placed her handbag next to it. Looking down the choices she fished in the bag, pulled out a lighter and a packet of cigarettes, flicked one into her mouth and lit it as the barman approached. Without looking up from the menu she exhaled smoke with her order of Jack Daniels and ice in a voice that made it clear it wasn't the first Jack Daniels she'd ever had, or the first cigarette.

Her monochrome look perfectly matched the dark and melancholic bar; black trouser suit, white blouse against white skin, and black shoulder length hair with a fringe framed a pale face that could have been beautiful, had she put in some effort. The effect was not improved by the fact her expression made it clear that such effort was beneath her and she didn't give a damn what you thought anyway. The only colour was the scarlet lipstick highlighting a mouth that hadn't seen a smile in a long time and matching nails that tapped on the bar, but not to any particular tune. Her crossed legs allowed the right stiletto to tap the air, keeping time with her nails, while the left shoe anchored the ensemble to the footrest.

When her drink came she picked it up with the hand holding her cigarette and located a place on the menu with her left index finger. She gave the order to the barman and only looked up when she folded the menu and handed it to him.

She looked away from me, to her right, surveying her fiefdom. Coming back the other way her gaze met her own in the mirror and she paused. You would have expected her to have straightened her hair, or checked her lipstick, but she did nothing. A pedant might have thought the look of disdain deepened a little, but she moved on, taking another sip of her drink as she did. By the time she saw me, coming across the room to sit next to her, the glass masked her face and all I could see were her dark brown eyes. That was enough.

The look she flashed me would have turned some mortals to ash, right there, but I was made of sterner stuff and kept moving. When she realised the outer defences had been breached she moved to DefCon2, and took the glass away from her mouth to reveal one of those sneers pretending to be a smile.

"Hi Mum" I said.

"What the hell are you doing here?" she sneered. So I told her.

I told her about the plan. How the false red light couldn't fail to stop the mail train. How all we had to do was to overpower the crew, and move it along to Bridego Bridge. It was then a simple case of loading the sacks full of money into the waiting vans, and away to the farm at Brill. When the dust settled, we would split up and live the rest of our lives in luxury. The plan was foolproof.

Until we found out that the train was a new model and the idiot Biggs didn't know how to move the damn thing. So Reynolds had to get rough with the driver. Now it wasn't just robbery; it was armed robbery, maybe attempted murder. I'm just a van driver. I'm not above bending a law or two in the name of personal gain, but not with violence. So I legged it, and now I'm in trouble and need help. Well, you always turn to your parents when you need help. The police are after me, but I could handle that. It was one of the few lessons Mother taught me. But the gang needed to know that I wasn't about to turn them in, even if the Postmaster General was offering a £10,000 reward. I needed somewhere to stay and someone to act as a go-between with Reynolds and Wilson.

I spoke in a hushed desperate voice, fearful that once again, she would turn me away. When I finished the sneer had softened. "Sure, baby. Stay at the hotel. I'll foot the bill, you don't need to worry. I'll go see Reynolds at Leatherslade Farm. Bruce and I had a thing for a while. I'll square it for you. Why don't you have a drink and tell me what you've been up to". All in all, it wasn't a bad attempt at a smile.

Three days I sat in that hotel room, ironically with a perfect view of the tracks, less than a mile from where we committed the "Great Train Robbery". Three days of sandwiches and cheap whisky. Three days of boredom and fear. Waiting.

Then it was over. Then I was free. A tap on the door, and "It's me, baby. You're in the clear." I rushed off the bed and threw open the door and there she stood, right hand on hip, left hand high on the door frame, trademark stilettos and dark suit. "Did you miss me?" I backed away as she stepped into the room, creating the room for one, two, three uniformed coppers and, last, Slipper of the Yard. I'm not sure who's sneer was worse, his or hers.

I looked at her open mouthed. "Why?"

"Ten grand, baby. Ten grand. Be seeing you", she lied.

I never saw her again.

The Journey

By Rebecca Ridgway

Every day I catch the 07.59 train from Leighton Buzzard to Euston. Day in, day out, week in, week out. The seasons change, people are born and die, the earth gets warmer. Every January, fares increase. Twice a year, the drivers strike. Nothing much changes. Every morning at 07.59 a small group of us gather on the platform, always in the same place, ready to board.

We have our own little patch of platform waiting for the second carriage along. In the great tradition of the British public, we politely ignore each other. Yet every weekday, we spend 48 minutes in each other's company before dispersing to our various workplaces. I know nothing about my fellow passengers, their lives, hopes and dreams, families, jobs. Occasionally I see one of them shopping in town and they look oddly out of context, as if they shouldn't exist outside the confines of the second carriage along on the 07.59. We are total strangers.

A young woman catches my train. She is in her mid-twenties, tall and slim and is always immaculately dressed, sipping a latte as she waits. Maybe she works in property or PR, a public-facing job which requires her to be groomed. Every morning she has the same routine: she plugs in her iPod until we reach Harrow and Wealdstone, where she whips out a small gold compact and checks her make-up. Last month I noticed a shiny ring on her engagement finger and she now leafs through wedding magazines on the journey. I saw her last week in town, looking at the window display at Ann's Bridal Room.

A fifty-something man boards the second carriage along. He likes the same seat and gets irritated if it is occupied. He wears a pinstriped suit and reads the Times, always completing the Su Doku. I imagine he works in middle management. Everything about him is dull and grey, except his mobile ringtone which gives a burst of Mission Impossible. His wife often calls him on his journey; she is called Sue. Last year he stopped getting the train and after two weeks, I realised he wasn't on holiday and feared he had been made redundant. Or maybe he was ill. I even scoured the Deaths announcements in the Observer in case he had met his maker. I don't know his name but there would maybe be a picture, or an announcement from 'Sue'. Perhaps he had got another job but in this climate, it seemed unlikely.Then after two months' absence, one day last summer he appeared back on the platform in the pinstriped suit. He looked the same and I am burning with curiosity to know what happened to him!

A scruffy guy in thick glasses always sits in 'my' carriage. He first appeared last summer and quickly became a daily traveller on the 07.59. As we pull away from the station, he puts away his cycling helmet and pulls out a laptop. I'm sure he works in IT. His iPhone is forever ringing and he talks technical jargon loudly, causing others in the carriage to tut. Sometimes he looks hungover and he sips coffee from one of those commuter's mugs from the 99p shop.

I have named the fourth member of our bizarre little group Ms Peacock for two reasons: firstly due to her vibrant clothes, like an exotic bird; secondly, because I've seen her in Peacocks furiously raking through a rail of sequinned leggings. She dresses outlandishly, favouring garish colours, thick make-up and lots of jangly jewellery. I can't put an age on her although she must be at least forty and is what Gran would have described as 'mutton dressed as lamb'. She looked a bit surprised for a few weeks earlier this spring and I decided she had had Botox. I once saw her in town disappearing into a beauty salon. I can't imagine what job she does, but it has to be creative or artistic. She always reads a celebrity magazine on the journey and at Euston is immediately swallowed up on the Underground.

So every day we have the same routine. We have never spoken, only once exchanged glances and eye-rolling when the 07.59 became stuck in a tunnel for forty minutes. IT guy became flustered because he couldn't get a signal on his phone.

Until disaster struck last week. The new timetable came out and to my horror, the 7.59 was no longer running. I couldn't believe it as I scanned the tiny print. Instead, there was the 07.46 or the 08.12. What would happen to us all? Would we be scattered to the four winds, my silent travel companions and I? They were so much a part of my daily life; I couldn't imagine travelling to London without the accompaniment of Ms Peacock's clashing jewellery or Pinstriped man's Su Doku musings.

I deliberated all weekend, finally deciding on the 07.46. The 08.12 would get me into work just a little late. I hoped the others would do the same.

Monday morning, I stood on the platform in the same position but 13 minutes earlier, feeling strangely out of sorts. None of my fellow travellers were there. This was it; the end of an era. I'm a creature of habit, as you may have gathered, and I hate change. Then from far away, I heard a jangle of bracelets, getting closer and closer and Ms Peacock came hurrying along in a fluster as if the 13 minutes less had ruined her routine. About a minute later IT guy appeared and took up his usual position as if nothing had happened. The clip-clop of high heels announced the arrival of Engaged lady, who was sipping a latte as if nothing was out of the ordinary. Five out of six!

Then along came Pinstriped man with a copy of the Times tucked under his arm. Our eyes met and his crinkled with amusement. Then something very strange happened. He nodded at me and smiled.

In Praise of Sand and Clay

By Damien Plummer

They say a house built on sand is often swept away,

Yet is not the fortunes of Leighton made on its sands, silts and clay?

As I lay down these lines I'll expose

Its native Geology, their modern usage and how

Our humble market town footnotes our Nation's History!

So far from the coast, land-locked, it seems to me,

Beneath the waves 120 million years ago is where we'd be!

Ambling from Leighton to Woburn along the 'Ridge'

Have you ever wondered what the 'greensands ridge' could possibly be?

Sandstone of greenish hue, a high mineral silicate

'Green': 'organic' we like our gardening and farming to be

What better source of Potassium for free?

Hard water is softened to a smooth 'purity' by its alchemy.

Scant 5 million years after, the titanic forces that formed the Alps

Gave birth to the next product rich in economic worth

Colloquially known by its first users as 'Fuller's Earth'

Kneaded into woollen cloth it absorbed all oil and grease

Modern day winch operators smear it on brake bands to affect the same release!

Decontamination of Man and Mammal, improbable but true!

Used by Civil Emergency Services and the Military against chemical attack

For hygiene: for cat litter trays, chinchilla dust baths there'll never be a lack!

Mixed with detergent in fly-fishing not to 'spook' the catch

It too can be deployed even for 'nappy rash' for your little girl or boy!

Against acne and burns apply this recipe;

Lemon mixed with rose-water and 'Fuller's Earth'

Do try, you'll see it works!

Swollen rivers carving channels to the sea

With relief dumped their silt at the mouth of estuaries

Scant 100 million years ago.

Its discoverer with an eye to fame affixed his name to this humble mud

For posterity due to his claim it's called 'Gault's' Clay.

This light coloured clay mixed with chalk

Charmed the Georgians and Victorians

Who pining for the Palladian ideal baulked at Plebeian red

Bricks made from our clay-pits, formed Ducal Palaces

Best known Buckingham's, present home of our royalty.

For more modest examples look closely along Grove Place – I state my case!

At last, I'll tarry a while after this brief sprint through each Sedimentary Age.

Now refresh, we stand on what we're currently best known for: our Sand!

So rare, so pure, our White or Silver Sand is
In classic 'Coals to Newcastle' twist
We even supply the Arabs who are surrounded by it!
Present uses? Filtration, Sport, Leisure, Building
Myriad and more, they're never ending!

But please, I ask, indulge me once more,
For one of the commonest uses of Sand is Glass:
Optical or Practical, in so many colours it's true.
But here is our greatest claim:
Each pane that adorned Paxton's 'Crystal Palace'
The Great Exhibition's monument to the Industrial Age
Was fashioned from glass made from our Sand!

Where there's Muck there's Brass is an adage that holds true:
One of our biggest Sand Quarries bears the name
'Garsides' one of our entrepreneurial Clans
So profits still accrue!

Spooky Narrow Gauge Railway

By Neil Cairns

It really was a terrible November evening. The wind was blowing strongly and the rain was coming down in thick sheets drenching everything in its path. It was late as the mayoral car passed along Stanbridge Road taking its passengers home after a civic function at The White House. The rear seat passengers were the Mayor and his wife.

Their driver was their son who ran a local taxi company and the 'mayoral transport' a second-hand London Austin taxicab. The windscreen wipers were struggling to keep the rain at bay and the view ahead was difficult as the car wended its way along the empty street. There was no conversation as everyone was worn out. The rain still lashed down and ran past the car in rivers down the gutters. As the car climbed the gentle hill out towards RAF Stanbridge, the headlamps picked out the shining steel narrow-gauge rails of the level crossing ahead. Once these railway lines had carried the industrial life-blood of the town in its huge sand industry but since WW2 most of this product had been transported by road. Today the little railway only ran at the weekends as the town's main tourist attraction, carrying keen young steam railway enthusiasts as well as being a renowned industrial museum.

Old Austin London taxicabs are not very fast vehicles but they were designed for town use. The driver mused on this fact as he peered ahead into the wet, soggy gloom ahead. Then he became aware of a slight movement near to where the railway exited the crossing and disappeared towards Pages Park, the railway's town terminal. As the taxi drew nearer he swore he could see a boy holding a red flag. He lifted his foot from the accelerator to slow the cab and to take a better look. Nothing was clear in the rain, but there in front of the taxi was a boy, about fourteen years old, walking out into the road waving a red flag; it was almost midnight.

The cab came to a standstill at the crossing. There was no other traffic or signs of life other than this very wet boy in rather scruffy clothing. The cab driver wound down the door's window to listen. He and his passengers could hear the unmistakable sound of an approaching diesel locomotive. Not a big one, but that of a Simplex loco of the old sand railway pulling a long train of full sand skips. The boy stood his ground on the crossing and the approaching train got louder. By now the rear seat passengers had begun to take notice of what was happening. They too were utterly amazed that a train was running so late at night. All of them were well aware of the use of this line almost up until the early 1970s, but this was 2009! No sand trains ran any more, there was no longer any interchange sidings with the main line at Billington Road. They had been an industrial estate for over thirty years now. What on earth was this boy and this train doing here?

Then the rain really began to fall so heavily that the wipers could no longer cope. The taxi's occupants thought they saw a train cross the road with a dozen or so skips. But then there was a terrific and horrific scream. The train had not completely crossed, the boy had disappeared. This was just too much for the taxi driver and his father. Both jumped out of the cab into the lashing rain to investigate. But as they both looked up, the train had disappeared. The level crossing was empty. They ran over to look down the line to see if the train was there. Nothing. Then they both noted that the white metal gates on each side of the road blocking off the railway were closed and still padlocked. Then, out in that awful November evening they hear a soft crying noise. It was a sobbing noise that sounded like a distressed woman. They both turned to see a shadowy shape huddled out in the road wearing a wet-through shawl. She was cuddling a fourteen-year old boy to her chest. There was blood on the rails near her feet. Then a big heavy goods vehicle could be heard in the distance. Both looked towards it but it turned into the industrial estate. Looking back, the woman and child had gone. Both of them were by now soaked to the skin and neither could find any sign of the shadowy shape on that crossing or of any blood.

They looked at each other and then ran back to the waiting cab. Once inside their wet cloths steamed up the interior and they sat silent for a while. Neither was drunk, neither had suffered delusions, nor did they believe in ghosts. The Mayor's wife had also seen the same scenes as they had, but she had stayed firmly in the dry cab.

Should they call the police? Would they be believed? The driver would certainly be breathalysed. Instead they went home to mull it all over.

Once in the dry, warm house the son went to the bookcase and picked up a copy of a book on the Leighton Buzzard Railway by a local author. To his surprise, he found a reference to an accident on that railway in the late 1940s where a boy who had just left school had died. He had been the flag-boy and as such sat on the front of the loco. He had jumped off at Stanbridge Road crossing in the rain, and once the loco began to cross he had jumped on again. He had misjudged his jump and fell under the loco wheels and was then caught in the driving chains before its driver could stop it.

His mother had been informed and she ran to the scene to cuddle her dead child.

They had indeed seen a ghost.

This story is taken from the opening paragraphs of chapter 12 of a novel based on Leighton Buzzard's very own tourist attraction " The Long Bustard Light Railway Story" published in March 2010. Copies are available from Pages Park Station shop, all profits to the LBNRG.

I love LB

By Hannah Simpkins

I watch the rain come down

Making the street lights glisten

Like candles on Christmas Eve

The shops are shut, fair boarded up

As I return from the pantomime

I remember the happy times

I've had in Leighton

A year ago, sometime around today

I unpacked my stuff and filled this empty flat

Silently wondering, who I'd be or where I'd go

It could have been a grand mistake

The worst I ever made

Moving to a place I didn't even know

Now here I am, one year on

This place has welcomed me

This quiet town has opened its arms
And found a friend a home

And when people ask, where I live
I kindly tell them, proudly saying
I love, LB

Our Town

By John Hockey

One week embracing mythology, the next taking in the symbols of a saint. Looking back, it all seems very intellectual, yet in truth my early encounters with Leighton Buzzard were just the first faltering steps on a romantic journey.

A chance meeting of two souls from nearby Dunstable at the Unicorn disco in Lake Street was where the spark was struck and thirty something years later the embers still smoulder. I like to think it was my virtuoso air guitar performance to Jo Jo Gun's 'Run, Run, Run' culminating in a chair-canting crescendo that first attracted my future wife, but in truth it was probably the barefaced lie I uttered. After a couple of sideways glances we moved nearer each other and got chatting.

"What do you do for a living then?" asked Julie, and without hesitation I said the first thing that came into my head.

"I'm a jockey," I lied.

Standing over six feet in my socks, we both recognised the silliness of this remark and a smirk played over our faces. Anyone with a rudimentary knowledge of the sport of kings knows that, if you are a smidgeon over five feet two inches and have the weight to match, you can kiss goodbye to a career in racing.

Thinking on my larger than required feet, I attempted to extricate myself from the tangled web I had woven and added what I hoped would be a liberating 'in one bound he was free' comment.

"I'm not the jockey you see on the telly you understand. No, I'm one of the ones that ride the horse when they're being readied. We're out of sight of the cameras so it really doesn't matter how big we are."

Warming to the logic of my theme I added the killer remark.

"Actually it's a benefit being tall and heavy at that stage because when the real jockeys get on board, the horses really fly."

A laugh, a shared white lie. On such innocent economies of truth are lifetime relationships forged.

But the romantic chase must follow custom and for our first date proper we moved on from dancing at the sign of the mythological beast to dine under the symbols of Saint Peter, namely the Cross Keys. By chance (and if truth be told the reason I chose that eaterie), I had been there the week before under sufferance with my parents. Imagine my barely concealed amusement and delight when, escorting the impressionable Julie into the dining room, the head waitress enquired "Hello, Mr. James, your usual table?"

Julie's face was a picture. How many other conquests had I taken there before? Would the waitress be comparing her with all the others and mentally placing her on a score sheet?

No matter. The evening was a success despite not knowing whether to start with the fork nearest or furthest from the plate and failing to impress my date by ordering whitebait 'off the bone'.

Our third sortie to the unusually named market town eight miles distant from where we lived saw us walking hand in hand down the Grand Union towpath on a summer's evening. Never one to let the grass or in this case the dusty asphalt grow beneath my feet, I ventured a somewhat chancy remark.

"When we're married, how many kids do you think we'll have?"

I can tell you now that if ever you want to stop a girl in her tracks that is just the sort of comment to make.

"Who said anything about marriage?" Julie asked, adding defensively "We've only just met and anyway, we're both off to uni – you to Manchester, me to Sheffield, so how's that going to work?"

"We will get married though, won't we?" I countered and wandered on ahead allowing the thought to hang in the still air and surround the subject of my thoughts.

Although the Unicorn has transmogrified into the Lancer and the Cross Keys now sports a black horse to oversee its less than saintly operations, the canal still flows sweetly twixt Linslade and Leighton and somehow signifies our own grand union, born so long ago.

Nowadays courting is a bit different. Today a young buck muscular meets a doe crepuscular and animal passions are roused on the rutting ground that is the High Street.

We never did have kids but we still live not far from Leighton and pop in frequently. Each time I glance at the former Unicorn or Cross Keys I can't help recalling the days when we met and I know very well why Julie and I will always regard Leighton as 'our town'.

The Bad Experience Bus

Marilyn Downton

There were two of us old ladies on the bus and we were soon talking, partly out of self-protection as the bus was full of schoolchildren packed with energy like springs released from compression beneath a heavy weight. The females gave vent to piercing screams every few minutes, and the males were deeply engrossed in noisy dialogue accompanied by explanatory gesture. We were in danger of having our hats knocked off; we could barely hear each other speak and wondered if by some means unknown we had been rendered invisible, so when a boy leaning round my seat and shouting across the gangway raised the volume an inch from my right ear I decided to protest.

"Excuse me," I said, "I need to tell you I have a not uncommon form of deafness: I cannot hear soft sounds, a few more decibels and I hear quite well but a few more decibels than that and it hurts, so please, if you could keep it down a bit, it would help."

The boy looked stunned. I doubt if he had noticed me until I spoke, and it was obvious he had not intended to be unkind but this is the crux of the matter: these were children in spite of their size. So why are they on the bus without someone to accompany them? It may have worked in the past but times have changed. It is hard on the driver and unpleasant for other adults on board. Some of these children were going upstairs, coming down then going back up again. The driver shouted for order at that but for the most part he had to concentrate on driving. He had either a flower behind his ear or a coloured transfer stuck to one cheek - I forget which. Was this also self-protection or an offering from the children?

These were unruly, not bad, children but surely they need someone with them or more guidance at least. Who should take responsibility for this? Does anyone know or care? A gentleman who boarded the bus told us, after the children alighted, that he has to carry them off the bus at weekends - and it is not difficult to guess the reason for that.

*

My next bus was different, and you could say the laugh was on me this time. The driver looked a little worried when I boarded as the bus was full of schoolchildren: no seats.

"Help," I said, addressing the children, "will I survive? What do you do with old ladies - throw them on the floor and stamp on them?"

Silence; but I noticed a few smirks.

A thoughtful child offered a seat and I thanked him but I was not going far and had things to carry and manipulate, so it was easier to stay wedged in the gangway where I was.

Then something peculiar happened, self-preservation again perhaps, and to my astonishment I was transformed quite suddenly into a stand-up comedian. I would not care to tell you some of the things I said - with gaps for giggles and smirks. They were not the usual sorts of things one tells children, and if I do tell I might get thrown off the bus myself.

But dammit, children are not interested in the usual sorts of things, are they? So, well I'll tell you just one thing I said when a girl looked out of the window, saw a family of attractive little black children and said how sweet they were. I told her that when I lived in the Caribbean a black man told me that when he first saw white folk he thought they were dead or dying. No harm in that though was there? And it's not that any of the things I said were really shocking, it's just that old ladies don't stand at the front of the bus and address children even in commonplace idiom - maybe they should. An older boy deeper in the bus, in order to avoid bags, books, and bodies in the gangway, climbed over the backs of the seats and came forward, either because he needed to get off soon and that was his only hope, or because he wondered what I might say next.

"I had a bad bus experience before," I told him, "but these children seem reasonable."

"They are all over thirteen," he said.

So the others had been, I thought.

"And they are trusted," he added.

Some children do have guidance then, I thought.

"On the bad bus experience," I went on, "the females screamed every few minutes for no obvious reason, and I mean they screamed - they were much worse than the males."

"That's about it," one of the boys on this bus piped up.

"I wonder why," said I, "this must be a different sort of school then."

And there was a sequel. When I passed a group of boys cycling around in a precinct one morning, one of them slowed down beside me and said: "Can I call you Nan?"

"If you want to," I said, "but my name is ... and my nickname is ... but if you want to, just call me: 'you'".

I don't know any boys in Leighton Buzzard so I presume he was one of those from the second bus. I haven't seen him again but I guess I might; I'm not sure though that I'm a very good Nan as it is.

We elderly know travelling on buses at certain times is hazardous except, curiously, in Malta where I lived for a time; teachers there said they felt Maltese children had been over disciplined and that they tended to be suppressed - no imagination and so forth.

Watch it, I thought.

We elderly try to avoid buses full of schoolchildren but it is not always possible, and the drivers, at least, need consideration, don't they? They need to concentrate on the road and keep our children safe, but I guess if they complain in the present climate they might lose their jobs to those who do not.

Wind

By Derek Hardman

Nobody knew from whence it came
But to Leighton Buzzard, it did.

In the water meadows
The tall grasses were the first to notice,
And pointed, as a warning, to where it was going.
The frightened, fallen, leaves rushed hither and thither,
Looking for their friends.
They found them in a corner, along Bell Alley
Playing ring-a-ring o' roses.

Litter redistributed itself, and a sheet of LBO newspaper,
Embarrased by the constant staring,
Took to the sky to look down on people.
Timbers in the Alms Houses moaned at being disturbed,
Whilst chimney pots squatted closer to the roofs, fearfully.

The wind, having arrived, stayed for a while,
Huffing and puffing, full of its own importance.

In the High Street, to stay upright,

Lowry figures leant forward.

Umbrellas were blown inside-out

Their bones revealed in one mad moment.

Hair, normally confined by laquer, now danced merrily,

As silly overcoats did their best,

To shake out the person inside.

The flagpole on the White House roof,

Smacked incessantly by the rope, stood aloof

But the flag on top crackled and cackled at the fun.

Dust and dirt joined forces, and cowered together,

Hiding in shop doorways along Bridge Street

The wind whistled and whined, oo'ed and ahh'ed

And then was gone.

Nobody knew where it went.

Leighton Buzzard, exhausted, rested.

The Wreck of the Flying Scotsman

By Vanessa Byham

Bill was a keen trainspotter. From the tall Victorian over-bridge that spanned the tracks at Leighton station he could see all the trains and note them faithfully in the dog-eared notebook he kept in the pocket of his shorts.

It wasn't a very good day for visibility, there had been thunder swirling around the valley and sometimes the spire of All Saints Church had been obscured by low cloud. His grandmother, who had no teeth and rather scared him, told him that this kind of weather often presaged an event of some kind. Even though the rest of the country had been enjoying a fine September day, Grandma Brown said, in Leighton the weather had been just like this the day war broke out in 1939.

Bill didn't know what 'presaged' meant but nothing bad was going to happen today, he was sure of it. He leant against the cold iron, just tall enough at ten to be able to see over the side. Before that, he'd had to rely on his brother to hoist him up. Now, most of the time, Jim was too busy with football. And girls.

Bill shuddered. He was never going to be interested in girls.

Trains were far more interesting. Some really good engines had passed underneath, smokeboxes gleaming, clouds of white steam pouring in a glorious wake. He was well pleased with his haul, there were several there that he'd never seen before.

His mother had said if he was late again, there'd be no treat tomorrow. A whole orange! Of course, he'd have to share it with Jim- but still... he could almost taste the sweet-sour burst of the fruit on his tongue...

Bill's jaw jutted. He might be only ten, with skinny legs and not much of a chest, but he was going to make sure he got his share.

There was a rumour that the greatest train of all, the Flying Scotsman, was coming through. Bill looked at his watch doubtfully. It might not come...

And then he saw a burst of smoke on the horizon. At the same time, thunder cracked, there was a great sizzle of lightening. The sky darkened to the colour of coal.

And still, the rain did not come.

The train came ever nearer. The Flying Scotsman! Even if he had to get soaked, he'd note the number and then, when they were eating supper in their little terraced house in Waterloo Road, just a few hundred yards away, he'd casually mention the fact.

Jim had never, ever bagged the Scotsman.

Lightning forked again. Bill remembered that you shouldn't be out in the open, but the train was nearly there. A few minutes and it would pass under the footbridge. Then he could pick up his bike and dash home.

A great crash of thunder, as if the earth itself was about to split apart. Bill could have sworn the bridge shook. Clutching the slick metal, he steadied himself. The train was still coming, but now he could see that something was wrong. It was travelling too fast, the wheels were scraping horribly on the rails, the carriages were swaying from side to side, madly, crazily. Bill couldn't take his eyes off the train. The engine was bucking like a startled horse. It was close enough for him to see the glow from the fire box door, the blackened and sweat-stained faces of the driver and the fireman, waving his arms, shouting, but the wind snatched his words away into the pall of fire and smoke that was shooting upwards. Then with a snap and a crack, the engine derailed, taking the carriages with it. The whole train folded like a concertina, dragging, smashing into the waiting room on the Up platform, demolishing the Dunstable line bay.

Bill stared in appalled fascination, knowing that he should move, that the over-bridge was next, that the tall columns that held it up would be no match for the giant engine, with its iron pistons and enormous wheels. The wind howled, thunder roared and lightning cracked again and again.

There was nothing, nothing anyone could do and in a moment, he would be swept away like a broken twig.

He thought of Granny Brown, sitting in the chair, knitting by the fire.

'This weather is a warning. Something bad always happens.'

No, Bill thought, no. Weather didn't make things happen. Men made things happen. Like the war. His Dad had said that. It was about greed and power and things that Bill didn't really understand.

'No!' His mouth opened in a shout, the word should have been swallowed by the clamour, the tumult of the wild wind, the crashing and striking and breaking of metal and glass all around him. But somehow it wasn't. Instead it was magnified into a great bellow of sound until he could hear nothing else.

And then – silence.

Hanging from his railing, Bill felt as if every ounce of strength had been wrung from him. He slid to the dusty ground.

"William Brown!"

Clumping footsteps up the iron stairs, the whole bridge reverberating. His mother, pinny still in place, blazing with anger.

"What are you doing! Supper's on the table. I don't know, standing around, looking at those blessed trains. Your brother was the same. Thank goodness he's past all that now. Well, I tell you, my lad," she took hold of his arm, half-dragging him to where his bike was standing. "Your brother'll have all the orange tomorrow night, that much I can tell you."

"But…" Bill strained over his shoulder as his mother marched him and the bike at a fair clip towards home. In his minds eye, he could see shattered carriages, broken glass and – worse-broken bodies. The wooden station buildings burning, the Dunstable line platform gone.

Above his head, the sky was still dark, but the storm seemed to have passed. The rain had not come.

Constant Beauty: Walking by Clipstone Brook, Spring 1995

by Gill Lyden

Winter! Winter! Do your worst,

for I have seen the spring buds burst -

and within your glassy prison the almond flowers' rosy glow

flinging banners of war at the blinding snow.

Cast again your freezing gauntlet,

for the sun's burning blades are unsheathed for battle

and now can be heard your icy death-rattle.

Today I trudge in a blazing waste of whiteness,

lit by those blades Heaven-forged of Nature's molten gold.

The honeyed notes of the blackbird as he flings his soul to the sky

create a bursting song in my heart.

Rejoicing with me as your end is foretold

and drowning the voice of your whining wind

which howls its reluctance to depart.

The hazel too, at the field's edge, knows your day is done.

Her catkins hang withered on slender branch,

her fruit soft-wrapped in budded womb ready for Autumn's table

For many a year has her beauty graced the hedge besides the ash-buds sable.

She will be there still

(when you arise from your Arctic tomb,

to freeze us again through your bitter night) -

ready to awaken for Spring's delight.

The Road

By Justin Nash

114 million years ago: a sudden rise in sea level. A strip of land running across from Norfolk to the Isle of Wight is under water. 65 million years ago: the sea has disappeared and been replaced by a flat landscape covered in chalk. 2.6 million years ago: the Ice Age arrives and with it the sequence of alternately warm and freezing cold periods that continue today. In Leighton Buzzard, a river now known as the Ouzel, was once a mighty river flowing under the glaciers, and during periods of warming a mighty torrent stripping the soil underneath it down to rock. It is now a pleasant dreamy river, flowing northwards down from the chalky solidity of the Chilterns. There is much evidence of the work of the Ouzel; from the terracing carved in the valley and the round pebble gravels left at a place now known as Corbettshill Farm. Throughout Southern Bedfordshire the action of water and ice has stripped off the layers of soil and chalk above to reveal the sands and rock deposited by the ancient warm sea of 114 million years ago.

6,000 years ago: Leighton Buzzard, like most of England, is covered in forest, a mixture of oak and hazel but this is about to change. The first farmers arrive in the valley and begin clearing the woodland for fields, not just to encourage open spaces for hunting, as their predecessors the hunter gatherers had done. Now the geology and geography of what will be Plantation Road comes into play. The soil is very sandy on this part of the Lower Greensand and it is not good for growing crops; it is better for feeding grazing animals. The Road is open land, dotted with trees, furze and bracken. The vegetation of the heath is also a source of fuel and many other useful things. 4,500 years ago: the first metal workers arrive and copper is followed by bronze. To show status and power and to appease whatever gods they believe in members of the local aristocracy erect two barrows to serve as their tombs. The barrows, not yet covered in turf and eroded by time are beacons to the bronze age traveller.

2,600 years ago: only two miles distant from the Road Roman and British travellers pass along the new roman road which will one day be known by the Anglo-Saxons as Watling Street. In the distance the people can see the hill, naming it with Celtic rather than Roman words and using a Celtic word for hill which will one day be taken by confused Saxon invaders and supplemented with the English word hill, leading to the name Brickhill, literally hill hill.

1,400 years ago and the ancestors of the English, the Anglo-Saxons, have arrived in the valley and have either replaced or merged with the local Celtic people. They leave their pots, shield bosses, brooches, beads and other burial goods in their graves on the heath, a sign that they are still pagans or not yet convinced Christians. As pagans, the people believe the goods will be needed for the afterlife. Some of the grave goods will later be seen, divorced from their owners and the purpose for which they were planted in the reddy soil, in the Wardown Park Museum in Luton and the British Museum. Another hundred years pass and there is a grand Christian basilica only three miles away at Wing and the time of preparing for a pagan afterlife is over.

1086, the Road is largely heath and partly the rich grazing land of a meadow running next to the county boundary. The counties have been introduced by the Saxons, with the right hand side of the river bank in Bedfordshire, the left hand side in Buckinghamshire. Near to the heath, two mills are in operation, using the power of the Ouzel to mill grain for the lord of the manor and the people of the town. The town now has its own church. Across the Ouzel, Linslade has been a separate manor since 966.

1164, Henry II gives the manor of Leighton, including the heath and meadow of the Road, to the Abbey of Fontrevault, the main church of an order of monks and nuns favoured by the Plantagenet kings. Land that will one day be under tarmac and houses helps feed, amongst other livestock, '4,500 sheep' in 1318. Although the Abbey will finally lose ownership of the manor in 1414, the heath continues to be a vital part of the town's economy. In the flood meadow next to the Ouzel grass grows with gusto, driven on by the regular winter flooding that still often turns the meadow into lake in winter with the Ouzel once again becoming the river of its dreams. A water birds' paradise, in the distant future of mobile phones and the internet keen dog walkers will have to change their path because of these mighty winter waters, and cattle will once again graze on these lush fields when the floods are ended, juxtaposed with the suburban havens of the Road.

Five hundred years pass. Leighton Buzzard is now pressing to expand into the heath. The track across the heath is known as Great Brickhill Road, as it leads, if followed directly, to a track leading past the Rushmere pond. Then it moves up through the steep wood-banked Bragenham Lanes and Ivy Road, to the ridge on which sits the village of Great Brickhill in Buckinghamshire. The medieval hunting park separated by pale by the Wars of the Roses magnate Lord Grey of Ruffyn at the top of the ridge is gone, now only distantly remembered through the calm title of 'Park Farm'. Heaths along with the medieval field systems of which they are part, are coming to the end of their long history. New ways have been found since the seventeenth century to feed livestock all year round. Plantation Road is about to be born.

Across from the Ouzel from 1800 a new artificial waterway, the Grand Junction - later Grand Union - Canal now passes through the meadow. On either side of the canal, trees and hedge marking field boundaries can be seen frozen and cleaved by the canal for generations until most are grubbed up by farmers with no need for these obsolete boundaries, whilst others live on as curiously straight tree lines marching from towpath to the Ouzel. Generations of those walking the canal path silently and subconsciously draw the straight lines to connect the hedge and tree lines of the interrupted fields. Swing bridges which once allowed people and farm animals across from Linslade will one day be allowed to disappear or gently rust, fetchingly daubed with the words, 'out of order' in red paint. Boats carry goods safely between London to Birmingham at unheard-of speed, with the capability to move a 20-ton load between the two in only 36 hours. 33 years later trains come thundering up the track, which often runs next to the canal, through the valley, at the terrifying speed of 25 miles per hour.

1848: the heath is divided up amongst the wealthy businessmen and landowners of town and country. Among their group is one member of a family of very wealthy local Quakers, John Dollin Bassett, whose family build all over Leighton Buzzard. It is now time for the heath to feel their touch. Large parts of the heath are planted with trees – including many foreign species such as giant redwoods - to fulfill the latest fashion for the exotic, a form of paradise which can still be seen all along the Road. This new forest, of which much still survives is known as the Plantation and by 1890 Great Brickhill Road has become Plantation Road. In amongst their 'paradise' the Bassetts' build mansions with names such as 'The Knolls' (named after the Bronze Age barrows in its back garden), and Heath House, which will not survive the twentieth century. Oxenden House, a mansion built by Thomas Saunt in 1912, will 61 years later be remembered only by its surviving lodge on the corner of Taylors Ride. During the Second World War Oxenden House plays a role in the training and running of the RAF's newly acquired radars and Heath House accommodates the Royal Army Medical Corps. A plaque will be left to commemorate the former outside the Swiss Cottage Nursing home but the wartime service of Heath House will only be remembered on paper.

With the birth of the 'Plantation' after 1848, come medium size and smaller houses at the southern end of the Road. Some were once substantial like numbers 21 to 31, once home of Albion, later Waverley House, now only commemorated by a grand wall with a lion gate in front of 1970s houses. Others have their names and dates of construction given on plaques, with 1872's Laburnum Terrace representing the end of most housing development at the beginning of the Road until the 1900s. With the beginning of the twentieth century the road's houses develop in fits and starts, with every decade adding to the mix. However, it leaves large areas of woodland, such as Heath Woods and probably the only street in England with giant Redwoods a common feature for part of its length.

Other businesses arrive along with the houses to add to the long standing farms. Plant nurseries and sand quarries, seed merchants, shops and garages come and go, until most of the Road has become a dwelling place for the workers, parents, children and pets carrying on the everyday task that is their lives. The Stag Public House from 1854 greets travellers at the town end of the Road and once seen stays in the memory. The Road is home to the old woman known in the 1920s as 'Old Granny Smoke a Pipe', who lives in a later to be demolished thatched cottage, near the now departed Avery's Garage (now Badgers Brook). She buries her clay pipes and then digs them up in the hope that they will be clean. Characters like this are part of a hidden history, unlike the buildings and geography of the Road. Their tales are the most elusive part of our story, leaving little trace outside chance survival in books, the Census and fading fallible memories. Even murders in the Road and its tributaries, one by a husband of his wife in the Great War, another in the 1940s of a woman in Firs Path will not be remembered other than in lurid books on Bedfordshire Crime sitting on dusty library shelves or in fading memories.

The story ends for now with a golf course. In 1925 part of the land previously owned by the Bassetts at the north end of the Road becomes the new Leighton Buzzard Golf Club. It had previously not been planted and remained virgin heath. This modern leisure pursuit notorious for transforming countryside into a countryside where nature bows down to man's feverish desire to manicure and control, includes in its golf course the legacy of the Road as a landscape partly made by man and once kept as heath by the grazing of generations of hungry farm animals. The 75th Anniversary brochure explains that 'the ponds on the 5th and 7th holes...are thought to be old cattle dips belonging to the Knolls Estate.' The old Road meets the new Road.

This Leighton Buzzard Hell

By Hannah Simpkins

Passing through the tunnel, headed home

The icy road descends the mountainside

Hell, there it is, I'm sure

Appearing over the brow

Staring back at me

Fog creeps round the edges

Spire standing tall

Glowing, effervescent

Submerged within it all

A town, some call it

But matters not

A welcome sign, a gate

A passageway

To the underworld

The streets deserted

Satan's carriages littering town

A neon glow of soulless shops

Selling pre-packaged lives

The still canal, water running dark

Ghost ships sailing through

Along the River Styx

This town

This Leighton Buzzard Hell.

The Great Little Train Robbery

By Neil Hanley

* * *

Leighton – Linslade Citizen Thursday 22 October 2009

Thieves once again broke into Leighton Buzzard's narrow Gauge Railway shed on Wednesday night.

The gang stole more engine parts from priceless stock which is disrupting the 90th anniversary celebrations. A standby train has been put on emergency use for the weekend.

* * *

"Smoke Daddy, look, smoke!"

I looked across at my youngest. His bright-eyed face said it all. He was excited. He had been looking forward to going for months. His deep fascination with trains had started with famous 'Thomas.' Now wherever he went, he sang the theme tune.

He loved trains.

My wife was at work. My eldest, Phoebe, was at her grandparents'. I had to take him. I had little choice. It was now or never. I had been assured that the risks had been minimised.

Ten other people stood on the platform that morning, shielding their faces from the biting wind. Red and yellow leaves littered the track, glistening in the fresh morning air. The train itself stood boxy and shiny blowing white smoke into the trees. I stood next to a young woman.

We clambered into the front car together. I held Freddie tightly. I wanted to make sure he was absolutely safe. The young woman wrapped in a scarf and thick fleece sat next to me. She immediately began talking with Freddie. She had an easy smile. Freddie pointed out of the window at the billowing smoke. She laughed. Freddie giggled.

Perfect.

I purposely sat opposite an elderly gentleman. I sized him up quickly. Angular face. Silver hair. Keen eyes. He sat hunched in the corner writing furiously on a small note pad. He wore a long thick sheepskin coat.

I glanced at the woman and casually thumbed my mobile.

Doors slammed. A shrill whistle. I opened my mouth and gave Freddie a look of surprise. He mimicked me.

"It's starting, Daddy!"

The driver powered up the 112 hp Dorman diesel engine. It rumbled into life powering the little train forward. Freddie squealed. We left Page's Park station, climbing sharply between the park and a former sand quarry, now full of houses.

The man seated in front leant across to look out of the window. His face beamed almost as brightly as Freddie's who watched fascinated as the train stopped at Stanbridge Road level crossing, to let off the flagmen to stop the traffic.

I took my chance.

"Isn't it fantastic?" I said to the man.

"Yes, marvellous."

I detected a Northern European accent.

I thought quickly, facts and figures bounced inside my head. 'A four wheel diesel-hydraulic, very nice.' A sideways glance at the woman.

"You know the Beaudesert?" The man's eyes glinted. He leant forward in his seat.

I nodded.

"One of my favourites," the man said. "It used many parts from an earlier 900mm gauge Simplex locomotive," he said beaming.

"Supplied to the National Coal Board in 1979." I added.

The man reeled off a further six engine models. I ticked them off in my head.

Priceless Data.

I responded with youthful enthusiasm. The journey continued onwards taking us along sharp curves, steep gradients, following the local geography, past Marley's Bank pushing onto Leedon Loop. There was always something around the next corner.

How true that was today.

Freddie clutched his free Rail Trail activity pack, whilst the woman pointed outside as the train pressed on through a green corridor of trees past more modern housing.

"You seem very knowledgeable about trains," said the man inching a little closer. "Do you follow them?"

"I like to read up on these things," I said guardedly. I pointed at Freddie. "It's educational isn't it?"

"I take trains everywhere very seriously."

I nodded thoughtfully. I'm sure you do.

I glanced out of the window. I had visualised the journey in my head. I knew we weren't far. We crossed Swing-Swang Bridge and began the long climb to Vandyke Road level crossing.

After a short while, the woman turned and looked across at me. There was an urgent look in her eyes. We were leaving the last of the houses the scenery was changing, opening up into wide green hills.

We were getting close.

I saw the track of an old sand quarry branch disappear behind the gardens.

The end of the line for us was near too.

I kept my eyes peeled outside. I couldn't force the situation. It was all about timing. I could just make out Chamberlain's Barn quarry in the distance, as the train began to climb to its highest point of the journey so far.

I had come too far to blow it now.

The Whipsnade Lion carved into the chalk hills was almost taunting me.

Do it now.

No, not yet. Wait.

I looked at Freddie all red cheeked. He needed to be made safe first. In case it got nasty. A screech of brakes tore me out of my thoughts. The Stonehenge Works station signed appeared just ahead of us.

I was ready.

The train began to slow, grinding steel threatened to scramble my brain, fuzz my thinking. The man stood up. But the woman was already there waiting at the door with Freddie in her arms. As planned.

A sudden jolt. A stumble. The train came to a halt. A loud click. The doors flung open. The woman stepped down with Freddie.

"...there's two, there's four, there's six, there's eight - Thomas and his friends..." Freddie sang.

I stood in front of the man. I could see the cavalry arriving on the platform. Freddie was being led to the safety of the station hut. WPC Marsh had done it.

I turned towards him. I flashed my badge. "Detective Hampson."

His eyes widened.

"Magnus Dataheim, I am arresting you for the robbery at Leighton Buzzard Railway. Anything you wish to say..."

At last, I had my man.

'Teresa of Watling Street': A view of old Bedfordshire

By Kevin Barham

If you drive up the A5 from Dunstable, on the brow of the hill just before you reach Hockliffe, you will see to the right of the road a lone house standing out clearly on the horizon. This house, Trinity Hall Farm, has one of Leighton Buzzard's famous literary associations for it was here that in 1900 the novelist Arnold Bennett came to live.

Bennett was 32 when he moved to Trinity Hall. He had won a literary competition in 'Tit-Bits' magazine in 1889 and had then taken up journalism full time. In 1894, he became assistant editor of the periodical Woman. Just over four years later, his first novel, 'A Man from the North', was published to critical acclaim and he became editor of the magazine.

He came to Bedfordshire because he was looking, not only for a country home where he could devote himself to full-time writing, but also because he wanted to have his elderly parents with him. He particularly wanted to look after his ailing father Enoch. Hockliffe was ideal as a novelist's retreat as it was sufficiently remote from the bustle of London, and yet had a good rail link with the capital at Leighton Buzzard on the London and North Western main line.

Bennett's time at Trinity Hall Farm had its moment of sadness. It was there that his father finally passed away. On 17 January 1902, Bennett wrote to a friend: "The Pater finished his course in perfect quietness at 8.40 last night". Enoch Bennett is buried in Chalgrave churchyard just four miles from Hockliffe.

Trinity Hall Farm is where Bennett completed his novel 'Anna of the Five Towns'. In his journal for Friday for Friday May 17th 1901, he tells us: "I finished 'Anna Tellwright' [his original title for the book] this morning at 2.45 a.m. after 17 hours continuous work, save for meals, on the last 5,000 words. I was very pleased with it; slept well for 4 hours, got up with a frightful headache, and cycled through Hemel Hempstead to St Albans, lunched at the George, and home – 42 miles".

'Teresa of Watling Street', written while he was living in Hockliffe, is Bennett's only attempt at detective fiction. It is an oddity of a book never destined to become a classic like 'Anna of the Five Towns'. Its main interest for Leighton Buzzard folk today is that Bennett sets the action mainly in Hockliffe and the surrounding area.

Teresa tells the story of Richard Redgrave, a young man hired to investigate Raphael Craig, a bank manager suspected of fraud who lives with his daughter and their servants at 'Queen's Farm' in Hockliffe. The farm is based on Trinity Hall Farm, although most of the other local names – Hockliffe itself, Dunstable and Leighton Buzzard – remain unchanged.

Bedfordshire was on the brink of change when Bennett was writing. Watling Street was still a dusty thoroughfare yet to be macadamed. But mechanical ploughs were already at work in the fields and Richard Redgrave drives back and forth between London and Hockliffe in an electric car. Strange as it may seem to us now at a time when we are looking for alternatives to the petrol-driven automobile, the early 1900s were the heyday of the first electric cars – "odourless and almost noiseless", as Bennett describes them. We can only wonder how many pedestrians were mown down when they failed to hear one coming.

How Bedfordshire has changed since Bennett's day. When his hero Richard Redgrave arrives in Dunstable en route to Hockliffe, "It was a warm, sunshiny, sleepy, day, such as suited that sleepy town, and showed off its fine old church and fine old houses to perfection". Who would recognise the town in the following description? "There is no theatre in Dunstable, no concert-hall, and nothing ever excites this staid borough save a Parliamentary election or the biennial visit of Bosco's circus".

On the morning of Redgrave's arrival, Bosco was in town "with his horses, camels, elephants, lions, bears, acrobats, riders, trapezists, and pavilions, encamped in a large field to the south of town". It must have been a very large field as we are told that the circus had two hundred horses with a tent capable of holding four thousand people.

Richard attends the afternoon performance of the circus (a fateful occasion for him as it turns out) and spends the evening in the Old Sugar Loaf Hotel in the High Street, an old coaching inn which still exists. At midnight he leaves the inn to drive to Hockliffe. He finds the circus is also leaving town, a straggling procession of animals and vehicles heading up Watling Street – "a weird and yet attractive spectacle". As he runs through the Chalk Hill cutting to the north of Dunstable, he finds the elephant herd standing in the road. It takes some stretch of imagination to imagine the scene as you drive down the A5 today.

Bennett had a fascination with Watling Street and its history and had tracked what remained of its route on a series of county maps from Kent through London and onwards. He was delighted that the road "flourished and abounded exceedingly in my particular neighbourhood as a right line, austere, renowned, indispensable, clothed in its own immortal dust". To him it was "a wonderful road – more wonderful than the Great North Road or the military road from Moscow to Vladivostok". He notes in Teresa that between Dunstable and Hockliffe "the surface of the road was perfect – for the Bedfordshire County Council takes a proper pride in its share of this national thoroughfare". He also says, however, that "Watling Street, like all great high roads, is infested with tramps".

The book contains frequent descriptions of the local landscape and landmarks. In addition to Dunstable and the Chalk Cutting, we are told about the chimes of the clock on Houghton Regis church. We also learn about the numerous chalk pits in the area. In one episode a circus elephant pulls a stranded motor car out of a pit. There are mentions of the Craigs catching trains at Leighton Buzzard. We hear that Redgrave enjoys speeding through the country lanes when he takes the Craigs to and from the station.

Bennett also gives us an impression of Hockliffe as it then was: "Now, the first dwelling in the village of Hockliffe as you enter it by Watling Street from the south is a small double-fronted house with a small stable at the side thereof. A vast chestnut-tree stands in front of it, and at this point the telegraph wires, which elsewhere run thickly on both sides of the road, are all carried on the left side, so as not to interfere with the chestnut-tree. Over the front-door of the house, which is set back in a tiny garden, is a sign to this effect: 'Puddephatt, Wine Merchant'. Having descried the sign, the observant traveller will probably descry rows of bottles in one of the windows of the house". Richard Redgrave rents a room from Puddephat's aunt at the other end of the village and dines in the White Hart (today a Harvester pub).

In the introduction to The Book Castle edition of 'Teresa', Bedfordshire writer and historian Simon Houfe tells us that Puddephatt is based on Arnold Bennett's main helper in the village, Arthur J. Willison. The latter was both a tailor and horse dealer at Hockliffe, although in the novel he appears as a wine merchant and horse dealer. With his knowledge of the locality and its gossip and scandals, Willison became an important part of the novelist's life in the village.

Bennett left Hockliffe in 1903 when he went to live in Paris. We don't know if he came back to Hockliffe before he died in 1931. But he has left us a tantalising view of the Bedfordshire countryside around Leighton Buzzard in the early 1900s, before pylons, housing sprawl and swathes of bright yellow rape invaded the landscape: "The day was jocund, the landscape smiled: in the forty-acre field below the house a steam-plough, actuated by two enormous engines and a steel hawser, was working at the bidding of a farmer who farmed on principles of his own, and liked to do his ploughing at mid-summer. The steam-plough rattled and jarred and jolted like a humorous and high-spirited leviathan; the birds sang merrily above it; the Chiltern Hills stretched away in the far distance, bathed in limitless glad sunshine; and Watling Street ran white, dazzling and serene, down the near slope and up the hill towards Dunstable, curtained in the dust of rural traffic".

Sources consulted for this story include:

Teresa of Watling Street, Arnold Bennett, (first published 1904), The Book Castle edition, Dunstable, 1989, and Introduction by Simon Houfe.

Letters of Arnold Bennett - Vol. I: Family Letters, (ed.) James Hepburn, Oxford University Press, Oxford, 1986.

The Journals of Arnold Bennett, (ed.) Frank Swinnerton, Penguin Books, Harmondsworth, 1954.

Leighton Buzzard in Twenty Ten

By Kate Allan

Girls with buggies, ladies with trollies

getting off the bus from Dunstable for

tea shops, charity shops, and 99p Stores.

Shops about to close, shops about to open.

Shops with sales, and bargains, and posters of ASBOs.

Mums with kids straight from school in Waitrose.

Matinee film crowd. Library users. Bank workers.

School leavers heading for Peacocks. Job Seekers.

Plush-hatted pensioners outside Boots. Daytime drinkers.

Red Lion, Black Lion,

Golden Bell, Top Bell,

Lancer, Litten Tree,

Roebuck, pastry shop.

School kids in white shirts off to Wilko's for sweets.

Sandwich boards from mews' shops in the streets.

Estate agents in suits with cups from Costa's.

Travel agents' windows with cruises and the Costas.

Teens from the nail bar, old men from the barbers,

young grannies weighed down with shopping,

busy as bees plough through Town without stopping.

A Link With Fame

By Mike Moran

What links the Tesco supermarket, by the Grand Union Canal in Linslade, and the Science Museum in South Kensington? A clue is provided by the design of the store's weathervane, which is of an old aircraft. There is also the name 'Vimy Road,' for this was not always given over to the retail trade and car parking spaces, but once represented an important part of Britain's war effort during the conflict of 1914-18.

On this site was located Morgan and Co, a coachbuilding firm which built cars using American-imported chassis, but something else was manufactured here: an aircraft, the Vickers Vimy.

The Vimy, named after the Battle of Vimy Ridge in 1917, was designed as a twin-engined strategic heavy bomber with a crew of three, to be used against Germany. The first prototype flew in November 1917 and early versions used a variety of power-plants, such as Hispano-Suizas, Sunbeam Maoris and Fiats, before the Rolls-Royce Eagle was selected as the standard engine for the new aeroplane.

Large orders were placed for the Vimy and Vickers sub-contracted a considerable amount of the construction work. One of the firms selected was Morgan.

The Vimy was too late to serve in the First World War. On October 31st, 1918, just eleven days before the Armistice, only three Vimys had been delivered to the Royal Air Force, and at the war's end contracts were cancelled, including that with Morgan's, where 40 aircraft had already been completed.

Nevertheless, the Vimy remained the RAF's standard heavy bomber until 1926, when it was increasingly relegated to training duties.

And the Science Museum? A visit to the Aeronautical Collection will show a biplane with the fabric on one side of the fuselage removed to reveal extra fuel tanks. This aircraft, with John Alcock and Arthur Whitten Brown as pilot and navigator, was the first aeroplane to fly the Atlantic non-stop, covering 1,920 miles. The aircraft took off from St. Johns, Newfoundland on June 14th, 1919, in good weather at first, but then a fog bank was reached and neither Alcock nor Whitten Brown could see the sky or the sea for seven hours. A 'window' in the fog allowed Brown to obtain star sightings to confirm their position.

The fog closed in again, and, worse still, the aircraft went into a spin from 4,000 feet and the plane came out of the fog 'close to the water at a dangerous angle,' in Alcock's words. He brought the Vimy out of the spin, and climbed back through the fog and by dawn had reached cloudbanks which the plane could not get above. The two aviators were in cloud for over five hours, suffering showers of hail and sleet. Finally at 11,000 feet, they glimpsed the sun shining through the clouds and Whitten Brown calculated the aircraft's position.

It was decided to descend, but the aircraft was practically at sea-level before clear visibility was reached. Eventually Alcock and Whitten Brown crossed the Irish coast and saw the radio station at Clifden, landed, unfortunately in a bog. The aircraft was badly damaged, though Alcock and Whitten Brown were not hurt. The flight had lasted 16 hours and 27 minutes.

Alcock and Whitten Brown were knighted and won the £10,000 prize offered by the Daily Mail back in 1913 for the first non-stop flight across the Atlantic. The Vimy was repaired and taken to the Science Museum, where it remains. Other Vimys were used on trail-blazing long-distance flights: in 1919, the brothers Keith and Ross Smith flew from Britain to Australia in 30 days; and the South Africans Pierre van Ryneveld and Christopher Brand used two Vimys for part of their epic flight from Brooklands to Cape Town in 1920.

The aircraft which flew the Atlantic was not one of those built in Linslade, but the town can take very great pride in producing a highly advanced aeroplane for its day which made history by showing that long-distance air transport was possible, and within ten years was a fact. Think of that when next you see the weathervane.

The Bombs Bombed Down on Leighton; Unfortunately for me

By Hannah Simpkins

The bombs bombed down on Leighton

Unfortunately for me

The bombs bombed down on Leighton

A quiet Sunday, just past three

Ladies sitting out, drinking tea

The grass was green and mowing

The sun glowing in the sky

Canal boats gently rowing

As the bombs bombed down on Leighton

Churning up the turf

Potatoes ripe for harvest

Hay sunny haymaking

Rabbits chomping carrots

Walkers quietly walking

Passing by the hours

I'd drunk my cup of coco

Polished off the cake

Licking my lips

And counting the ticks

Of the old grandfather clock

The house had been a happy house

Where children play and laugh

Sleeping through the parlour games

The fire now burns so bright

All this really doesn't matter

For what came next, was last

Out of nowhere, out of sight

The bombs bombed down on Leighton

Destroying the summer grass

Peace remains

No one left

Just quiet air in Leighton

After the bombs have passed

Trying on Knickers in Peacocks

By Mark Norwood

It was all that Rachael's fault really. It had been two weeks since I split up with Darren and she said it was about time I stopped moping around and copped off with someone else. I agreed, reluctantly at first, but the more I thought about it, the more a night on the town in MK appealed.

What didn't appeal were my skanky panties. Why are they always grey? I'm sure I've bought loads of sexy knicks over the years but whenever you go out to pull all you can find are nasty, old lady pants, grey and crusty.

By the time Saturday came I was proper up for it, so's I had to get me underwear sorted. My E.M.A. is only ten quid a week and me dad is too much of a stingy git to cough up any panty money. It's alright for Rachael, she gets thirty pound E.M.A. but I suppose that's cos her mum can't work anymore after that accident with the hoover attachment.

Peacocks it had to be then. Sexy pants that don't last five seconds but are cheap cheap cheap. Now I know you're not supposed to try knickers on properly in shops, but I really can't stand knickers that crawl inside your bum-crack. New knickers have to pass 'the test'. So I slip off my nasty pants and slip on these black lacy jobs with red trim. I jump up and down and up down, wiggle wiggle wiggle, thrust thrust thrust. They didn't show any signs of being eaten by my arse. Bend over, bend over, bend over. Whoa!

As my head went down the third time it felt like it carried on going. Although I was standing still, bent over, I felt like my whole body was dropping like a stone. Falling on the outside and rising on the inside. I had instinctively closed me eyes. When I opened them the world had changed. I was still in a kind of booth but there were no hooks with me clothes on, instead there was a TV screen and the curtain had been replaced by a wooden door. I stood there for a moment wondering.

Okay right. Well it had been months since I'd tried smoking that Salvia, but was this some kind of flashback? This was different though, it was real. The Salvia had just made me sit in the corner thinking I was a chip and hoping that no-one would dip me in some tomato ketchup. This was something completely different.

Fuck it, I thought. Does it really matter what's happened? Life's too short; I've always been one for grabbing whatever comes my way by the horns. So I opened the little wooden door and stepped outside.

FOOOM! The heat hit me like when I worked in the bakers on a Saturday, until I got sacked for gobbing in that old biddies' roll. Busy busy busy. It was still Leighton Buzzard sort of, only bigger, taller and more complicated. There were still bits and bobs of buildings that I recognised but they had all been added to. There were repairs, alterations and extra storeys. Wooden towers added to the tops of buildings, giant screens flashing pictures on their sides, little windmills. People, people, people everywhere. Most of them bald and none of them wearing much in the way of clothing. I stood there in my T shirt and knickers not looking altogether out of place. The sun screamed down at me and I realised I was covered in sweat. In fact the whole place stank of sweat. As people rushed by all around me I got whiffs of hundreds of different B.O.s, sweet, savoury, sour, one just like sausages, another beef pie.

"Hey. Niiiiccce wig!" One of the endless bodies stopped. And what a body! Just the right amount of muscle, wearing a pair of speedos that had something wrong with them and a bald head. He smelt of sunshine and sugar puffs with just the slightest suggestion of chinese takeaway. Gorgeous.

"Sod off. This ain't no wig," and then he grinned a grin that had me instantly.

"Course it isn't. Next you'll tell me you don't want to come to my mates' party."

Yeah, so I wound up at his mate's party. He lived in a flat in this massive wooden building where Tescos should be. I mentioned this at the party but no-one seemed to have heard of Tescos.

The party was proper brilliant though. Loads a people there, all in knickers and no hair except for the odd wig. I had got used to the constant smell by then. I danced danced danced and so did my new 'special friend' Kieron. Then weird shit happened. He sat me down on this sofa and gave me what looked like a wooden cigarette. He had one too.

"Do you want it?" he asked.

"You got a light?" I replied. He laughed at me.

"Just put it in your mouth."

So I did, and so did he. It was cold at first put then got warmer and warmer. It moved in my mouth, growing, sending out roots. The roots coiled around my tongue, between teeth and probed my gums. It should have been repellent but instead it was sensuous, sexy, downright horny. Everywhere that the roots touched, tingled and the tingling grew more and more intense and began to spread back from my mouth down my throat into my body and up into my head. The end of the stick slowly swelled before breaking open. The petals of what looked like a flower made of paper spread and grew. It snaked its way to meet Kieron's flower which came to meet it. They paused before intertwining.

My whole body was throbbing by now, I felt like I was a pulsating beacon of light in danger of blinding everyone in the room. These were the best drugs I have ever done. My pulsing grew faster and ever more intense until the star I had become went supernova plunging me temporarily into darkness. I opened my eyes, there was a stick in my mouth and Kieron was grinning that grin again.

"Come on, lets go upstairs, there's something I want to show you."

YES! I thought, first great drugs and now for the great sex. He led me into this cosy little room.

"Just wait there a second." As soon as he was gone I whipped off my T-shirt and dropped the Peacocks knickers, their work was done.

He was back seconds later holding what looked like an empty, elderly Tescos carrier bag. As soon as he saw me his jaw literally dropped. His face was a picture of horror as a shaking finger pointed to my brazilian.

"What the fuck is that!"

I'm not having this I thought, so I grabbed his speedos and yanked them down. There, where his cock and balls should have been was just a thin faint scar with a little flap towards the bottom.

"Shit! I sooo wanted to have sex with you"

"But we just had sex downstairs, what more do you want"

"Listen mate you are one fucked up bunny and whats with the stupid bag?"

"Me mate's dad found it when he was a kid. No-one had ever known what it was before but what you were saying earlier jogged my memory."

I started crying crying crying. Me mum worked in Tescos before she died.

We'd like to take this opportunity to thank Leighton-Linslade Council for the grant to develop and promote this publication and to the following friends and supporters of Leighton Buzzard Writers:

Leighton Linslade Town Council

Bluebell Day Nurseries

Loobi Crafts

Nigel Crump Photography

Derek Hardiman

Mrs J B Hanley

Mrs M G Plumber

Marian Ridgway

Mr M Moran

Mr K Barnham

John Hockey

Mr and Mrs J Nash

Claire Fisher

Kathryn Holderness